TAKING THE CAT'S WAY HOME

"Jan Mark has created another super novel for early readers... This thoughtful story may give some children inspiration and hope in dealing with bullies."
The School Librarian

Jan Mark is one of the most acclaimed authors of books for young people. She has twice been awarded the Carnegie Medal and has also won the Guardian Children's Fiction Award, the Observer Teenage Fiction Prize and the Angel Award for Fiction. Her many titles include *Taking the Cat's Way Home*; *Thunder and Lightnings*; *In Black and White and Other Stories* and *They Do Things Differently There* (shortlisted for the 1994 Whitbread Children's Novel Award), as well as the Walker picture books *Fur*; *Strat and Chatto* (winner of the 1990 Mother Goose Award); *Fun with Mrs Thumb* and *This Bowl of Earth*. Jan Mark lives in Oxford.

Paul Howard has illustrated a number of stories, including *Friends Next Door*; *A Very Special Birthday*; *Jim's Winter* and the picture book *Rosie's Fishing Trip*.

D1180941

Books by the same author

The Dead Letter Box

The Twig Thing

For older readers

Dream House

Handles

Nothing to be Afraid of

Thunder and Lightnings

Picture books

Carrot Tops and Cottontails

Fun

Fun with Mrs Thumb

Fur

Strat and Chatto

This Bowl of Earth

JAN MARK

Taking The Cat's Way Home

Illustrations by Paul Howard

WALKER BOOKS
AND SUBSIDIARIES
LONDON • BOSTON • SYDNEY

For Hamid and Nafeesa
J.M.

For Ted and Eric
P.H.

First published 1994 by Walker Books Ltd
87 Vauxhall Walk, London SE11 5HJ

This edition published 1995

2 4 6 8 10 9 7 5 3 1

Text © 1994 Jan Mark
Illustrations © 1994 Paul Howard

This book has been typeset in Sabon.

Printed in England

British Library Cataloguing in Publication Data
A catalogue record for this book is
available from the British Library.

ISBN 0-7445-3667-7

Contents

Chapter One

Jane's cat was called Furlong.
People said, "What a strange name
for a cat," until they saw him. Then
they understood. Furlong had a face
and a tail, two ears and four feet.
The rest was fur. You could hardly
see his legs.

Kind people said, "What a fine cat." Rude people said, "That's not a cat, it's a feather duster."

William, at school, said, "That's not a cat, it's a loo brush," but that was not the worst thing he did.

Andrea never said things like that, because she liked Jane and she loved Furlong. Andrea lived next door. She was one year older than Jane, so they were not in the same class at school, but they were friends.

"I can remember when you were born," Andrea said to Jane. This was not true, but she said it sometimes so that Jane would remember that Andrea was much older. Jane could not say that she remembered when Andrea was born. Even Furlong was older than Jane.

Every day Jane and Andrea
walked to school together, on their
own, because there were no roads
to cross and lots of other people
were going to school as well.

Jane's mother said to her, "Don't
step in the road. Don't talk to
strangers. Never let anyone give
you a lift." She said it every day as
Jane went down the path.

Then Andrea came out of her house and they walked together along the street, every day. Every day, Furlong went with them.

First of all he ran in front, and when he got to the corner he sat and waited for them. When they turned the corner, he ran to catch them up and walked beside them.

When they turned the last corner, Furlong ran on ahead and sat by the school gate until they got there too. Jane and Andrea stroked him and said goodbye.

Then they went in to school and Furlong walked home by himself. Jane thought he walked back the way they had come, but he did not. He had his own way home.

Everyone knew Furlong, all the people in Jane's class and all the people in Andrea's class. The teachers knew Furlong. So did Mrs Giles, the caretaker, and the lollipop lady. Mrs Kumari, the school secretary, knew Furlong because one wet morning he put his muddy paws on her new pink skirt. Jane was afraid she would be cross, but Furlong smiled in his fur and purred, and Mrs Kumari forgave him.

Everyone knew Furlong except William.

William was new.

Chapter Two

One morning Jane and Andrea were
saying goodbye to Furlong when a
new dad and a new boy came along
the street.

"What a fine cat," the new dad said. This was the proper thing to say to Furlong, but the boy just glared.

Jane looked at the boy and the boy looked at Jane. He put out his tongue and made his eyes go funny.

When Jane went into her classroom the new boy was there with Mr Singh. Jane liked Mr Singh because he was kind and he had lovely whiskers, like Furlong.

"This is William," Mr Singh said.
"He is going to be in our class. Who
has an empty space at their table?"

Jane sat with Matthew and Habib
and Alison. There were two empty
spaces at their table. "Don't put up
your hand," Jane said to Alison.

She remembered the face that
William had made when he saw
Furlong. "We don't want him here."

But Matthew and Habib put up
their hands and jumped up and
down, so Mr Singh sent William to
sit on one of the empty chairs.

He sat down opposite Jane and made his eyes go funny again. Then he kicked her, under the table.

At break time William went off with Matthew and Habib and they all stood together under a tree and whispered.

When it was time to go in again, Jane looked at William's chair and said to Alison, "Will you change places with me?"

"No, I won't," Alison said. "I don't want him making funny eyes at me."

When everyone had come indoors, Mr Singh said, "Now, get out your News books."

He gave William a book to write his News in.

William wrote, "My name is William."

He looked at Jane. Then he wrote, "I do not like cats," and turned his book round so that Jane could see what he had written.

Jane wrote, "There is a new boy at our table. He does not like cats. I do not like him."

Habib leaned over and said, "Why don't you find another table to sit at?"

"Yes," said Matthew. "We don't want any girls on this table, do we?"

They had never said anything like that before.

Chapter Three

Next morning Jane said to Mum, "I
don't want to go to school today."

"Do you feel poorly?" Mum asked.

"There's a new boy at school,"
Jane said. "He doesn't like cats."

"Lots of people don't like cats,"
Mum said. "You will have to get
used to that."

"He doesn't like me, either," Jane said, but she still had to go to school.

She walked down the road with Andrea and Furlong. Furlong ran ahead, and sat and waited, and walked behind, and then overtook them and ran to the school, just as he always did.

People stopped and said hello to Furlong, and Furlong purred and waved his feathery tail.

Then William came along, without
his dad. He did not say hello to
Furlong. He leaned down and said
"Sssss!" very loudly, and Furlong
jumped away. No one had ever said
that to him before, not even Mrs
Kumari when he put mud on her skirt.

William said "Sssss!" again, and
Furlong was frightened. He jumped
on to the wall of the house by the
school and his fur stood on end
because he was angry.

"Leave my cat alone," Jane said.

Andrea said, "If you do that again I'll tell Mr Singh, and he will make you stand in the corridor."

"That's not a cat," said William. "That is a loo brush." Then he picked up a stone and threw it.

The stone did not hit Furlong but it scared him. He jumped on to the top of the wall and ran away, under the trees.

"I hate you!" Jane shouted, and hit William. William hit Jane, and Andrea ran inside to fetch Mr Singh.

"I can't have you fighting," Mr Singh said when he came out.

"She hit me first," William yelled.

"He threw a stone at Furlong," said Jane.

"Go inside at once," Mr Singh said. He was angry. Even his whiskers looked angry.

When they got to the classroom he said, "William, you are not to throw stones at *anything*. Go and sit down." William sat down and kicked Alison under the table.

"Now, Jane, stop crying," said Mr Singh. "You ought not to have hit William, even if he did throw a stone."

"But Furlong was frightened," Jane said. "He ran away. He'll get lost."

"I don't suppose he will," Mr Singh said. "He's a grown-up cat and he knows his way about. Which way did he run?"

"He went along the wall by the school field," Jane said.

"Well, then, he was going the right way," said Mr Singh. "You live in Kemp Street, don't you? Cats have their own way of getting around. They don't have to walk in the street, like us."

Jane went to her table.

"Tell-tale. Tell-tale," William hissed.

"Tell-tale," said Matthew and Habib.

"I'll get you tonight," William said. "After school, I'll get you."

After school William's dad came to meet him.

"I'll get you tomorrow, then," said William.

Jane and Andrea ran all the way home and when they got there Furlong was sitting in the garden, washing his toes. Mr Singh was right. Cats have their own way home.

Chapter Four

When Andrea and Jane and Furlong
walked to school next day, William
was waiting at the gate.

As soon as Furlong saw William,
he jumped on to the wall. William
did not even have time to say "Sssss!"

"Loo brush!" William shouted instead. Furlong turned round and ran away along the wall beside the school field.

"I don't care," Jane said loudly. "Cats have their own way home."

"Tell-tale," William said. "I'll get you after school."

"I'll get you after school," William said, at break.

"I'll get you after school," William said, at lunch time.

"William's going to get you at home time," said Matthew and Habib at afternoon break.

At home time Mr Singh told them to go. William went out quickly with Matthew and Habib, to lie in wait for Jane.

Jane stood at the gate with Andrea. William's dad was not there today,

but they could see William's head
poking round the corner, at the end
of the road. When William saw Jane
and Andrea, he hid.

"He's going to get us," Jane said.

"No he isn't," Andrea said. "We
won't go home that way. We'll go
home the way Furlong goes."

She climbed on to the wall of the house by the school. It went up like steps until it was as high as the wall by the school field.

"Quickly," Andrea said. "Here comes William."

Jane climbed on to the wall, walked up the steps and followed Andrea.

William and Matthew and Habib
were already running down the street.

Andrea began to run and Jane
ran behind her, along the wall. Then
they stopped.

"Did they see us?" Andrea said.

"Where are you?" William
shouted, in the street.

They could not see him and he
could not see them.

"I can see you!" William yelled.

"He can't," Andrea said. "He thinks
we're hiding by the gate. Come on."

"It's a long way to the ground,"
Jane said.

"Don't look down," Andrea said.
"Walk slowly. We need not hurry
now. Pretend you are walking on a
tightrope."

Jane did not think that this would
help.

"I know where you are! I'll get
you," William shouted, far away.

Jane thought how silly he must
look, and she felt better.

Chapter Five

On one side of the wall was the
school field. Mrs Giles was pushing a
machine up and down, making white
lines on the grass for sports day. She
did not see Andrea and Jane.

On the other side of the wall was
a row of back gardens. They passed
a garden full of roses and a garden
full of rubbish. Things looked
different from the top of the wall.
This is what birds see, thought Jane.
This is what Furlong sees.

Next they came to a garden with
an apple tree at the end of it. Jane
knew that tree. It hung over the
field and in autumn people picked
up the apples that fell from it.

Now the apples were small and
green, Jane and Andrea had to step
carefully over the branches.

Then they met a white cat sitting
on the wall. It would not move.
They had to step over the cat, too.

In the next garden was a prickly bush. It scratched their legs and Jane was afraid that they would fall into it, but they got past the prickly bush. In the garden after that, two people were sitting in deckchairs. One of them turned round and shouted, "Oi! What are you doing up there? Get down at once!"

"Run!" said Andrea, and they ran for seven whole gardens, over branches and through prickly bushes, along the wall.

At last they came to the end of
the school field.

"We must turn left here," Andrea
said. Now they were on the wall
that ran along the end of the
school field. There were no trees
in these gardens and they could
walk quickly.

Then Jane said, "Look."

Mrs Giles was not in the field any more, but over by the school was William. Matthew and Habib had got bored and gone home, but William began to run. Far away William shouted, "Now I'm going to get you!"

"He's seen us," Andrea said. "Quick. When we get to the next garden, turn right. There's a big tree to hide in."

It was a very big tree with very big leaves. It stood in a corner and four walls met under it, like a crossroads.

"This way," Andrea said, and they ran along a wide wall, out of the tree.

"Turn left," Andrea said. "Turn right. Turn right again."

They stopped running and looked round. They could not see the tree, or the school field, but they could see William.

Now William was on the wall as well, but he was going the wrong way.

They stood quite still until he was out of sight. He was still shouting, "I can see you!"

"We're safe," said Andrea.

"We're lost," said Jane.

Chapter Six

They stared all round. Jane was right. The gardens looked different from the top of the wall, but the houses all looked the same.

"Our house has a window in the roof," Andrea said.

"My house has a creeper growing up it," Jane said.

They looked and looked, but most of the houses had windows in their roofs, and a lot had creeper growing up them. They sat on the wall and wondered what to do.

"Let's go back," Jane said, but they could still hear William shouting far away, and they did not know how to go back.

"Mum will be waiting. She'll be cross," Jane said, and she began to cry.

"Don't be a baby," Andrea said, but she knew that her mum would be worried too if they did not get home soon.

"There is a swing in our garden," Jane said, and they looked again. There were five gardens with swings in them.

"We've got a shed," said Andrea. All the gardens had sheds.

"I wish we could find a policeman," Andrea said, but there were no policemen walking on the walls, only cats.

Jane watched the cats and then she had an idea. She stood up and shouted, "Furlong! Furlong!"

"Don't be silly," Andrea said.

"It's not silly," Jane said. "I have a special voice for Furlong. He always comes when I call." She shouted again. "Furlong! Furlong!"

They waited, and waited.

Nothing happened.

"Try once more," Andrea said, and Jane called again. "Furlong! Furlong!" Then Andrea stood up and pointed. "I see him."

Far away a ginger cat was running
along the wall towards them, waving
his feathery tail. He came closer and
closer. It was Furlong.

He ran up to Jane and put his
muddy paws on her skirt. Jane
stroked him. "Good
Furlong," she said.
"Now, take us
home."

Furlong knew
the way. He ran
along the wall
and then sat
down and waited for
them to catch up with him.
He turned left and
they followed
him. He turned
right and they ran

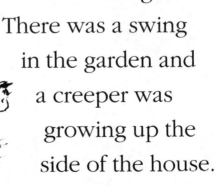

behind. He jumped on to the roof
of a shed at the end of the garden.

There was a swing
in the garden and
a creeper was
growing up the
side of the house.

The house next door had a
window in the roof.

Jane's mum was taking the
washing off the line. When she saw
Jane and Andrea on the wall she
dropped all the washing.

"Where did you come from?" she
said, and ran to help them climb
down.

"We've been taking the cat's way home," Jane said.

Then they heard William's voice again, but William was not shouting now. Far away, William was running along the wall, and William was crying.

William called, "Mum! Mum! I'm lost! Dad, I'm lost!" William had no cat to show him the way home.

"Who is this?" said Jane's mum when William reached Jane's garden.

"It's a poor little boy who has got lost," Andrea said, loudly.

Jane's mum lifted William down from the wall and led him indoors.

"Tell me where you live," Jane's mum said, "and I will take you home."

She walked down the street with William and made him hold her hand.

Jane and Andrea stood at the gate and watched. They did not say anything, but they smiled.

And Furlong, in his long fur,

smiled too.

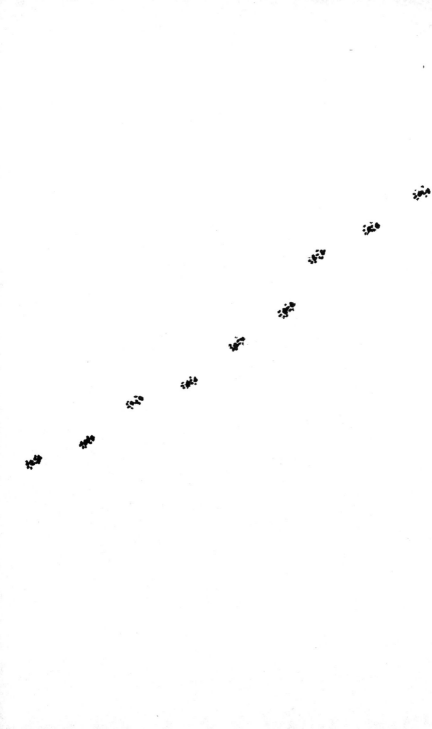

MORE WALKER PAPERBACKS
For You to Enjoy

☐ 0-7445-3183-7   *The Baked Bean Kids*
                by Ann Pilling/Derek Matthews   £2.99

☐ 0-7445-3668-5   *Impossible Parents*
                by Brian Patten/Arthur Robins   £2.99

☐ 0-7445-3665-0   *The Biggest Birthday*
                Card in the World
                by Alison Morgan/Carolyn Dinan   £2.99

☐ 0-7445-3664-2   *Gemma and the Beetle People*
                by Enid Richemont /Tony Kenyon   £2.99

☐ 0-7445-3666-9   *Beware the Killer Coat*
                by Susan Gates/Josip Lizatovic   £2.99

☐ 0-7445-3095-4   *Millie Morgan, Pirate*
                by Margaret Ryan/Caroline Church £2.99

☐ 0-7445-3188-8   *Beware Olga!*
                by Gillian Cross/Arthur Robins   £2.99

☐ 0-7445-3092-X   *The Snow Maze*
                by Jan Mark/Jan Ormerod   £2.99

**Walker Paperbacks are available from most booksellers,
or by post from B.B.C.S., P.O. Box 941, Hull, North Humberside HU1 3YQ**

24 hour telephone credit card line 01482 224626

To order, send: Title, author, ISBN number and price for each book ordered, your full
name and address, cheque or postal order payable to BBCS for the total amount and allow
the following for postage and packing: UK and BFPO: £1.00 for the first book, and 50p
for each additional book to a maximum of £3.50. Overseas and Eire: £2.00 for the first
book, £1.00 for the second and 50p for each additional book.

Prices and availability are subject to change without notice.

Name   _____

Address   _____

_____